"Lutzke has a way with words that merges horror and compassion in a single sentence. Reminiscent of Robert McCammon."

~ Joe Mynhardt, Crystal Lake Publishing

———

"Lutzke's rich, descriptive stories always leave me wanting more. He's a gifted wordsmith."

~J. Thorn, best-selling author

———

"Chad Lutzke has an awesome grasp of descriptive writing...Brilliant malevolence! He is a true master at his craft."

~Blaze McRob, Bram Stoker Award nominee

———

"Lutzke is a student of the horror genre with a rich voice that needs to be heard."

~ author, Terry M. West

———

"Lutzke's writing is personal, detailed and often heart breaking in a terrifying way."

~ Matt Molgaard, Horror Novel Reviews

———

"Chad Lutzke is an emerging and exciting dark author with a firm grasp on the genre. His shadows have drastically different heartbeats, unique souls, but are unified by their dark charm and bleak shrouds."

~Zachary Walters, The Eyes/Mouth of Madness

———

"Chad Lutzke is an excitingly fresh emerging voice in the horror scene. His writing pulls you in, and his stories are chilling and stay with you well after a thoroughly satisfying read!"

~Nicholas Grabowsky, Black Bed Sheet Books & author of HALLOWEEN IV

———————

"This man is a genius when it comes to writing a book. He is not just an author. He is a storyteller in the truest form of the word."

~ Nev Murray, Confessions of a Reviewer

———————

"Chad's writing is a trip to the buffet of horror. No stone left unturned."

~ Blaine Cook, vocalist for The Accused, Toe Tag, & The Fartz

Wallflower

by

Chad Lutzke

Dedicated to those who have tried filling a void.
And to those who have never recovered.

Prologue

There are the curious, and then there are the dangerously inquisitive—those of us who reach beyond a morbid interest and into something morally questionable. Something that will pacify a nagging itch in our psyche if only we dive in head first. Without thinking. Without rationale, to experience for ourselves what we can't understand by merely gawking at the ugliness from afar. Like a toddler to the seductive dance of a candle's flame, the need to touch what we're told not to. That's the kind of dangerous curiosity I'm talking about. The kind that dumbs us down, allows us to reach out and take hold of that which will hurt us. No matter the cost.

That was me. I needed to know.

1: Temptation

It was late summer and had barely rained all year. But Texas is like that so I can't bitch. It comes with the territory. I'm not sure there's anywhere on the planet you can have lush grass and authentic Mexican within a hundred miles of one another.

I had just spent a few days away from home over at a friend's place. Dad hated that. He'd made it pretty clear he never wanted me around but then would throw a fit when I stayed away for more than a day. So when I got home, Dad was ready to lay into me about everything and anything. He'd have these moments–quite a few of them, actually–where he'd remind me about my future, about having no job and about how he was going to charge me rent if I didn't at least go to community college. "You'll be just like that Miller kid," he'd always say to me. Marcus Miller was a guy I went to school with. He ended up in prison for raping his cousin. Apparently Dad thinks not having a job fresh out of high school is a gateway to sexual deviancy and perversion.

I usually just take it, let him mouth off, get it all out. But this time I spoke up. I told him that with any luck I'd be the complete opposite of him.

"The hell is that supposed to mean?" he asked me.

I told him it meant that if I ever did have kids I'd love them, not berate them. I'd support them, not ridicule them. And that if I ever had a wife that I'd love her too. And not cheat on her. Dad didn't see it coming. He didn't know I knew. When he left my room he slammed the door so hard it splintered the frame and cracked my bedroom window.

Hanging around there the rest of the day wasn't an option so I left for Boden's, a pool hall the gang and I would frequent. The gang—myself, Eddie and Kent. We'd all just graduated and spent most of our first summer staying up night after night in drunken states, fueled with the cheapest beer Corpus Christi had to offer. It made for a helluva hangover but left money for the next time.

We were still on our post-high school honeymoon. And with no job comes no responsibility, comes no money. Actually, Kent did have a part-time job at a pet store and had saved enough for a beater. Eddie had plans for college–or maybe the military, he hadn't decided–and me, well my mind wasn't made up just yet. Dad wanted college for me, of course. Mom didn't care either way. She just wanted me gone and married, working somewhere, *anywhere.* Just so long as I was providing.

But it's not unheard of for someone my age to take a year off or so, to think things over. I wasn't worried. I'd never been in any hurry to get to adulthood, so this next year I wanted to revel in my youth. In the meantime, I'd rely on Kent for rides. And for beer money.

That summer, when we weren't at Boden's playing wannabe hustler, we spent a lot of time with urban exploration—venturing into abandoned buildings like houses, old theaters, factories or even the old folk's home on 20th Street. It made for fresh environments to linger for the day. And the sense of danger, that feeling of not wanting to get caught but knowing if you did you'd get nothing more than a scolding. I mean, who hasn't lifted a private fence and slithered under or climbed through the broken window of a deserted building? I've a hard time thinking any cop coming across us in the middle of one of our ventures wouldn't just shoo us away, cracking a nostalgic smile, reflecting on days long past.

But then again, a local boy in blue went and broke three of John Matthews' ribs and an arm down at the 7-Eleven just for not turning his music down when asked—a scuffle I'll never forget. The snap of John's bones when he hit the pavement, all 250 pounds of Officer Ditmer crashing down on him.

So, one afternoon, while losing hard to a drifter in the pool hall, Kent was handing the shark a ten from his malnourished wallet, when Eddie came back from the vending machines holding three bags of chips and three cokes.

"Check this out," Eddie said. "So, last night I'm talking to Jen's friend Angela…"

"The one with the tits?" Kent holds out his hands cupped over his chest.

"Yeah, her. Anyway, she says her little brother and his friends went out to Limewood and ran into a squatter…some junkie living in one of the townhouses. Scared the piss out of them. They took off, thinking they'd get raped or something."

"Like Andrews," Kent said, looking at the floor and shaking his head, giving Andrews condolences for his deflowered anus and the stitches that followed.

"Yeah, like Andrews. Poor kid." Eddie paused and gave the same sympathy but with a wincing look of pain. "Anyway, we should head out there, check it out."

"And do what?" I asked. "I mean, we've been out there a hundred times. Every house is the same, gutted. What's some vagrant gonna do for us?"

"I dunno, man. I guess we'll find out when we get there."

"Sounds fun," Kent said, "but there's like fifty houses out there."

"Angela said the house was all the way in the back and the garage has a big black fly painted on it. Should be easy to spot."

With zero idea on why we should head to Limewood, both Eddie and Kent were convinced it'd be a good idea, and by late that afternoon we were driving down I-37 with the last bit of Kent's money sloshing around in the tank of his Honda Accord.

***

Limewood was an abandoned housing development that lost its funding just before completion after the man in charge went to prison for defrauding. The bank caught on and things were shut down immediately. All the homes had already been built but the insides lacked electrical wiring, and only half held drywall; the other half nothing more than timber skeletons sporting attractive siding— alluring warts across the dried skin of Corpus Christi, Texas. Other than the tall meadow grass, from I-37 the houses looked livable. But lack of curtains on the windows—the ones still intact—and sporadic graffiti told those who visited that every building was indeed abandoned.

Kent pulled the car off from the freeway and onto the cement drive, which ten feet later gave way to a faint path that ran throughout the development. The lack of trees added to the uninviting appearance, and the tall grass bowed low in the wind as though waving us away, that there was really nothing to see here.

"All the way in the back somewhere," Eddie said.

Kent followed Eddie's directions and drove slowly along the path.

"Right there's the one where those guys built the skateboard ramp inside." Eddie pointed to a house that contained more graffiti than the rest. A large circled "A" painted haphazardly in red spray paint took up most of the garage-door canvas, while various band logos surrounded it. I recognized some of them from patches I'd seen on the punk kids at school.

Once at the end of the path, Kent stopped the car. "Left or right?"

"I dunno. She didn't say," Eddie said.

All three of us looked down each path, squinting, studying each townhouse.

"Big black fly, right?" Kent asked. "That way, all the way down at the end, on the left."

Kent turned and drove down the rugged path. The last house on the left sported a large fly with unusually straight edges as though done with a giant stencil. Kent parked right where a driveway would have been, as though he lived there. It seemed like the logical place to park. It's not like parking on the path would make things any less obvious—that people were out exploring property they shouldn't be on, maybe adding to the local artwork. Or like my friends and I, tossing a few back while gabbing on about school and girls. But this time we were there for

13

something different. Something I'm not sure any of us really understood.

Kent shut off the car and turned to Eddie and me. "Well?"

Neither of us said anything. We all knew there was no reason to be here. To be in search of Bigfoot made more sense.

"We should take a weapon, arm ourselves." Eddie said.

"A weapon?" Kent said, a shocked look at Eddie. It surprised me a bit, too.

"This guy's a junkie. Who knows what he's capable of. He could knock you in the head with a brick, grab your wallet and do some funky business on you while he's at it."

"At the risk of sounding paranoid, I think Eddie is right." I said. "Just for protection."

Kent sighed and grabbed the keys from the ignition. "There's a tire iron in the trunk, maybe a bat, too."

We got out of the car and Kent unlocked the trunk. He was right. There was a bat in there, an aluminum one. I grabbed it and Eddie grabbed the tire iron. I saw a hammer lying in there so I pointed it out to Kent. He said he didn't want it, then called us pussies.

We headed toward the back of the house. All the homes had sliders in the back. And from our experience, the ones that weren't busted out were all unlocked, which made for easy entry. As we walked along the home, a gust of wind penetrated the broken windows, creaking the gutted building and causing an unsettling whistle, like the whisper of a banshee.

As we turned the corner to the back of the house, the three of us stopped. Someone had hung a black sheet over the sliding glass door from the inside. The thought of the squatter just feet from us on the other side of the glass was alarming—spread out on an old, holey mattress, a needle hanging from his arm, perhaps even dead; his skin cold and blue and stinking. Or maybe he stood in another room, a brick in hand, waiting for strangers to enter his home where raping and bludgeoning would commence.

"Ready your weapons, men."

"Seriously, Eddie?" Kent said, as he looked around nervously for last-minute protection, like a stone or a stick.

As we crept closer to the slider, the wind died completely. There was an uncomfortable stillness and the rustle of the long grass fell dead. Our creep slowed to a near standstill.

"This is gay." Eddie said. He moved forward quickly, grabbed the slider door and pulled. It didn't budge. "It's locked."

"Let's try one of the windows." Kent said.

At this point I really began to wonder about our motive, the attraction of seeing a rundown junkie caught in the act. They aren't exactly anomalies. The world is full of addicts, and we'd seen our fair share of cachectic suspects lingering around the darker areas of town. I guess since it was all taking place on our old stomping grounds we thought we'd gained the right to witness the depravity within.

We walked back around to the side of the house. The windows were all intact, except one that had been covered from the outside by a weathered piece of plywood. Without saying a word, Eddie stuck an end of the tire iron under the wood and started to pry it off the building. The wood over the iron split and cracked as Eddie continued to pry it away from the house. The noise was ridiculously loud under the circumstances and I ducked my head down as a result, as though trying to hide. If anyone *was* inside, they could definitely hear us now. I didn't like the idea of breaking in like that but found myself with my fingers scooped under the wood and tugging at it, adding to the impossibly loud cacophony of splintering wood and screeching nails.

After Eddie pried at several areas around the sheet of wood, it hung like a flap by the nails above. I held the wood open enough for someone to slide through and waved for Eddie to enter. He took a peek inside first then hoisted himself up over the windowsill and into the room, the tire iron clanging on the wooden floor.

Eddie stood with weapon in hand and waved us in. I went next. Once Kent had climbed in, we all stood silent for a few moments, listening. My body tingled, nerves shooting through me. I suddenly had to piss. It felt like the first time I'd ever done this. I guess in a way it was. Every building we'd ever entered we did it with the assumption they were empty. Now, here we are entering a house we've been told has an occupant. Not a legal one, but someone calling it home nonetheless. Someone quite possibly strung out on drugs, and maybe just desperate enough to mean us harm.

Kent spotted an empty wine bottle on the floor and picked it up, holding it by the neck as a weapon.

"Pussy," Eddie said.

Kent frowned and mouthed for him to shut up. Most of the walls in the house were finished except for paint. Drywall hung securely on all but one wall, which divided what was most likely the kitchen from the dining room. At first glance there was no sign of anyone living there, at least not on the bottom level. We crept through the house, being careful not to step on debris that lay on the floor—loose nails, scraps of wood, empty bottles and a few candy bar wrappers. We checked the living room and kitchen as well as a few closets that acted as nothing more than doorless alcoves.

On the far end of the kitchen was a closed door. We stood quietly outside it and prepared to enter. I choked up on my bat while Kent raised the bottle above his head. Eddie played around with the tire iron, trying to decide whether he should jab with the pointy end or treat it like a club with the socket end. He settled on the club. After what seemed like much too long, I reached for the door, turned the knob and opened it.

The smell hit us before we saw it—the first sign that there was someone living there. Eddie stepped back while Kent ran, gagging along the way until he rested, covering his mouth on the far wall of the kitchen. A large five-gallon bucket, once filled with paint, evidenced by the thick, white drips on the outside of it, now half full of human feces and urine, sat at the end of a short closet-type room most likely what would have been the laundry room. There weren't quite as many flies hanging around as you might think, considering it was summer. And there had to have been at least two to three weeks of bowel movements in there, assuming the user was feeling regular.

Eddie started to laugh, holding it in the best he could, while Kent caught his breath against the wall.

"And there we have it, folks. Five bucks in gas and an afternoon wasted so we could take a peek at Junkie Joe's john." Eddie said.

I'll admit, as disgusted as we were, it did help break the tension and would have had me laughing pretty hard had I not been scared of being heard.

"You guys need to shut the hell up!" Kent said.

"There's nobody down here," I said.

"Well, if they're upstairs they can probably hear you."

"Why dump in your own house when there's a whole field out there?" Eddie said.

"Doesn't like the weeds tickling his balls?" Kent said.

"Let's get upstairs," Eddie said. "And shut that door before we all get hepatitis."

I shut the door and we headed toward the staircase, which stuck out in the center of the living room, unfinished and without rails. Surprisingly, the stairs didn't make a sound as we ascended them. Eddie moved first, then me, while Kent lingered on the first few steps. Once Eddie made it near the top he stopped. I think I heard him gasp, and I'm sure if I could've see his face I'd have taken off running, right behind Kent. Eddie stuck his arm out behind him, signaling me to hold off. He then waved us away and slowly stepped back down the stairs. When we reached the bottom, Kent and I were all ears to Eddie's frantic whispers.

"There's a person up there, just lying there."

"Guy or girl?" Kent asked.

"I think it's a guy. Could have been a chick, though."

I asked Eddie if he thought the person had seen him and he said they hadn't. He said he thought they were sleeping, maybe passed out.

"Maybe dead," Kent said.

"I wanna see." I started up the stairs and Eddie followed. Kent lingered. I made it up about as far as Eddie had and stopped. Across the hall, at the top of the stairs, was a person lying on a stack of cardboard, layers at least six inches high, in what would have been a bedroom. The person had on bright red shorts, a white T-shirt and dark hair. But that's all I could make out.

I took one more step and leaned in, squinting my eyes. At first I thought it was a girl because of the long hair. I took another step. And another. By this time I was standing on the top step looking straight ahead into the room. It was a man. He could have been forty. He could have been sixty. It was hard to tell. It was clear that life had taken its toll on him. His face was narrow and scruffy, and his hair curly and unkempt. He lay flat on his back and his mouth was open, his lips dry and cracked.

I took another step forward so Eddie could see. I turned and saw Kent trying to peek up from a few steps below. None of us were holding our weapons up; they were down by our side. There was nothing threatening about the sight of the man, and if it weren't for his slow and steady breathing I would have bet my life we were staring at a corpse. His skin was yellowed and pale, his eyes sunken, and of course his gaping mouth.

I looked around the room. In the corner was a clothesline that held a pair of pants, underwear, socks and a plain black T-shirt. There was a folded blanket on the floor next to the bed, and next to that was a cardboard box acting as a nightstand. On top of it rested a short stack of books, several pencils, a drawing pad and a bright orange plastic tray—the kind you'd find at a fast food joint. On the tray was a spoon, a lighter, a candle, a few syringes and a small envelope with what looked like a black strawberry stamped on it. Next to the table was another smaller box full of trash. There was organization to all of it. What little the man owned he took care of and liked to keep things tidy. From my understanding of a junkie, that was pretty unusual. The messy bucket downstairs now seemed out of character for him, and the care taken in his room helped give some humanity to the sickly man lying there.

"If he's dead I want nothing to do with this," Kent whispered.

I took a few more steps and by this time was at the room's threshold, looking down at the man. A plethora of questions went through my head. I wanted to know the guy's story. I could tell at one point he was probably a real looker, with his chiseled jaw and long hair. There were traces of him in the room that reflected who he used to be—the books, the pad of paper.

Without knowing the man before me, and with no personal experience with drugs harder than the occasional joint, I was naive about most of it. And it puzzled me to no end why someone would give up everything they had just for a high. What was it about heroin that someone would sell their body, neglect their kids, lie and steal. My mind searched for reason and there was none. Not from this angle. I'd even been thinking about it on the drive over. But seeing the guy lay there as though dead, unaware of three strangers watching him as he floated in some cerebral nirvana, got me thinking even harder. About how I think it takes a certain someone to fall victim to its clutches, to become a slave to something like heroin. People who maybe were on the verge of giving up anyway. And then heroin just acts as the catalyst to start the beginning of the end, like they subconsciously wanted in the first place.

But that's not me. I'm content. I'm grateful. And as far as I'm concerned, once I'm out of Mom and Dad's I've got a pretty bright future ahead. I got it in my head that the drug wouldn't take some people the way it did others. I started thinking that if I ever tried it that it'd be a one-time deal, just to kill the curiosity, to answer the questions that now plagued me. What does it feel like? And why be a slave?

"Okay, we saw him. Let's go." Kent whispered.

To everyone's surprise, Eddie leaned in with the tire iron and tapped the man's foot, both of which had missing big toes. The man didn't move.

"He's dead, man. OD'd," Kent said, this time no longer whispering.

"I can see him breathing, Kent," I said.

"Maybe it's a coma...a drug-induced one."

Eddie tapped the man's foot again, this time directly on the flattened stump where his toe should have been. Nothing. I walked slowly and quietly around the makeshift bed and to the box nightstand. I took the bat and lightly knocked the stack of books over just enough to see the titles of all three. There were two small paperbacks and a large hardback, like a coffee table book. The hardback was an illustrated compendium of flowers. The two paperbacks were both written by Richard Brautigan: A Confederate General from Big Sur and In Watermelon Sugar. I'd read neither before but did recall seeing a Brautigan book on my father's bookshelf, something about fish in America.

I noticed two of the walls in the room were white, while the other two were gray, with a television static-like appearance, but I couldn't tell why. As I looked closer, I saw that tiny flowers had been drawn in pencil over the entirety of the two grayed walls. There must have been thousands of them from ceiling to baseboard. This wasn't your average graffiti. This was unhealthy dedication. An obsession.

"Cut it out, Eddie." Kent said.

I looked at Eddie. He was still tapping the man's foot. Still no movement.

"You guys ever know anyone to try this stuff?" I pointed toward the orange tray.

"Nope," Kent said, no longer trying to remain quiet.

Suddenly the man shot straight up and sprayed vomit toward Eddie, who caught quite a bit of it on his shirt. Kent immediately ran down the stairs, two at a time I'm sure. I moved away from the bed and back over by Eddie who reacted by swinging the tire iron hard at the man, striking him in the ankle. There was a loud cracking sound. I was sure something broke. Eddie called the now-screaming man a pig junkie and threatened to steal his stash to pay for dry cleaning. Eddie's never dry cleaned a thing in his life and certainly not a pair of jeans and a T-shirt—a kneejerk reaction I suppose.

The man tried opening his eyes, a near worthless effort. His mouth slung open in a long frown, eyebrows raised, but his lids would not comply. He squinted at Eddie, then wiped his face and said: "Take it. I don't care. Take it all." Then he fell back hard against the cardboard stack, moaning. I'm not sure he was even aware how bad he'd been hurt. No doubt he'd feel it when the drugs wore off.

"I think we should bail now," I said.

Eddie stared hard at the man, then at his vomit-spattered clothes. "You give me AIDS or something, man, I'll come back here and set this place on fire, with you in it."

"Eddie, chill out, man. Let's go," I said. I think he'd forgotten we were on this guy's turf, invaders. As we left the room I looked at the guy's ankle. It didn't look right, already swelling and changing color.

We left the room and went back down the stairs, Kent had his pecker out and was pissing on the walls and floor, shuffling along, covering as much territory as his bladder would allow. I'd seen Kent do this before. It was kind of his thing, trophy pissing. But under the circumstances I thought it was distasteful.

"Really, man? This is someone's house, Kent."

Kent started laughing and Eddie would have too if he wasn't busy cussing his way through the window, pissed off about the puke on his shirt. Kent and I joined him outside and we all lit up a smoke, like it was just something you do after being a dick. Eddie took off his shirt and wadded it up in a ball and threw it on the floor of Kent's car. Kent complained about it. Eddie told him to shut the hell up, and then all was quiet for the next several minutes as we made our way back to town. Finally, Eddie started talking about how you can't get AIDS from puke but probably other stuff, like hepatitis or an infection. He said his aunt was a nurse and he'd ask her, said he'd tell her some homeless guy puked on him downtown. He kept on like this until Kent interrupted him.

"You didn't have to club him like that."

Eddie thought for a moment, looked at Kent, then looked out the window at the miles of dead Texas field grass along I-37. "Maybe not. Maybe I should have pissed on him."

"Not cool, man," Kent added.

"It was reactionary. I didn't know *what* was going on...scared the hell right outta me."

"Still, man. I think you broke his foot." Kent said.

"You wanna go back so I can apologize? I probably did him a favor. He'll end up going to the hospital, maybe get some help for his junkie problem."

"Whatever helps you sleep at night."

I stayed out of the conversation and let them go at it. It was moments like this that I wondered why they were my friends. We just weren't on the same level anymore, and I felt like I was the only one who was aware of it.

I never said a word to Eddie or Kent about my curiosities concerning heroin. Never saw a reason to, but I could tell even before we left Limewood that I'd be trying it. And that I would come back from whatever heaven-turned-hell others had visited, unscathed.

2: Succumbing

I laid in bed that night thinking about the guy in the townhouse and how he had given his life for a high, for something so temporary. How every waking moment was spent chasing something he'd never catch up to—the only future ahead filled with a bleak existence based on a daily decision that was stuck in a decaying groove. I couldn't really pity the guy, though. He'd done it to himself and he chose to remain.

Sleep wouldn't come so I hopped online and searched all things heroin until the birds threatened to wake before I made it back to bed. Most of what I researched was what to expect as a first-time user. It seems there were a handful of experiences I could go through, but consensus said I'd most likely get sick yet still enjoy it. I even watched a few videos of people shooting heroin or high on the drug. Some of the people just sat there, seemingly unaware of their surroundings, while others seemed to fidget. It didn't make a whole lot of sense how enjoyable something would be if all you're doing is lying there, unable to move. Again, there's something else at the root of why those who tried it got addicted. Something psychological. Something I didn't have or needed to worry about.

While researching, my main concern was my well-being while under the influence, and of course a short recovery time. I would not fall victim. I would not become a slave. Before I tried it, there was one more thing I wanted to do: Speak with someone who had personal experience. The next day I'd be heading back to Limewood, make a peace offering, and hopefully learn anything else I needed to know.

***

By noon the next day–with money I had left from graduation–I was headed downtown. Hillcrest to be exact. An area I never thought I'd find myself in, in particular all alone. My dad let me use his car. It was no big sacrifice on his part. He had two of them; one that would otherwise be sitting in the garage, adding to the oil stain under it. I told him I was putting in some job applications. He told me to take my time. Too easy.

Once downtown, on the corner of Van Buren and Washington, I saw two women who were most likely prostitutes, exaggerated hip swinging, tight-fit clothes. Even in the early afternoon they were out, taking the funds of horny businessmen on their lunch. I wouldn't say I was particularly intimidated by either of the women, but I did single one out that looked a little less threatening than the other—frail, dark circles under the eyes, a real poster child for street life.

I parked the car a half a block away and walked to the corner. I asked the junkie girl if she knew where I could score some "H." I'd seen the term being used online. I became concerned that maybe I had that tourist look, like I didn't belong—a potential target for being ripped off and given cut product (another term I learned) or even robbed of my money. I tried to act tough but without arrogance. I didn't want spit on my burger, ya know?

The woman asked me if I was a cop, then she asked if I wanted to party. I told her that I did and that's why I was looking for the H.

She laughed and said, "Nah, honey, you want me to get you off?"

Embarrassed, I told her no but thank you and then went back to my tough guise and said "Can you get me the goods or not? 'Cuz I can go somewhere else if not."

She gave me a dirty look, then asked if I wanted tar. I'm sure the look on my face told her I didn't know what I was doing. I was the perfect victim for whatever her or her dealer wanted to pull. I told her I wanted the tar, for two. She smirked and told me it'd be forty bucks, then said she'd be right back and went around the corner and through a green metal door, into one of those brick buildings that had the fire escapes you see in movies, where the bad guys make a run for it and the cops chase them out the window and down an alley.

I waited there on the curb as cars drove by, each passenger taking a long, hard look at me as I stood uncomfortably in a part of town that couldn't wait to eat me alive. Under my breath, I told myself to grow some balls, then I stood up straight. It helped, for a moment. Then the girl came back and asked for the money. I handed her a couple twenties and she slipped two tiny balloons into the palm of my hand.

"You'd best leave now." She said. "I wouldn't be surprised if you didn't make it out of here with the rest of your money *or* that tar."

I played it cool and tried to chuckle, continuing to act like none of this was new for me. She wasn't buying it. I thanked her, then tried to walk fast—but not too fast, like the old folks in the mall before the stores open. Once back at the car, I opened my hand. The balloons were both red, and when I pinched them they had small globs inside like clay. I didn't open them. I wouldn't have been able to tell if it was really heroin anyway. I'd save that for the junkie. As far as shooting it—for the most part—I knew what to do. But I wasn't going to do it alone. It was time to go to Limewood.

I took the balloons and put them in a zippered pouch I used to hold drafting pencils at school. Inside the pouch I'd put two brand new needles I stole from my dad. He used them for insulin. I wasn't worried about getting addicted, but I'll be damned if I'm going to stick a dirty needle in my skin. I also had cotton balls, a lighter, and a spoon. As far as I knew, I was prepared.

As I drove down I-37, I thought about everything I'd read online—people's experiences, their boasts, their regrets, and their warnings. There was nothing I'd done that ever led to addiction. Or even close to it. I've smoked pot. I've gambled and walked away when ahead *and* behind. Even a pack of cigarettes lasted me a good week. And with the exception of drinking on the weekends for the sole purpose of inebriation–not because I needed to–everything I ever did was done in a healthy and moderate manner: TV, food, spending money, pornography. Even when the doctor prescribed me Vicodin for a sprained ankle I stopped taking it before the script ran out. I was strong willed, self disciplined. There would be no problem. I would maintain control.

No doubt from the perspective of my friends, the idea of buying heroin from a whore in Hillcrest with the purpose of shooting it up with the man we'd attacked yesterday and bringing him a dose and a small bag of groceries as a peace offering would seem nothing short of insane, or stupid. But I focused on feeding my curiosity and the humorous tale I'd one day tell.

I pulled into Limewood, drove to the back, turned right. Scared of being spotted, I drove behind the house. I could hear the dead grass tickling the underside of the car, metal whispers telling me to turn back. I parked and sat looking at the back of the house. Nothing had changed. The black cloth still hung. I looked at the upstairs windows, which were all intact. I couldn't tell which side of the house his room was on. I tried mapping it out in my head and guessed the window faced the front.

I grabbed my zippered pouch and the small bag of groceries I brought from home—a few cans of coke, two honey buns, some granola bars, and beef jerky. I wasn't sure how the guy was eating but thought he could probably use the food. I got out and shut the door quietly, then made my way toward the loosened plywood, expecting it to be nailed shut again. It wasn't.

What if Eddie had killed the guy?

It didn't seem likely with just a hit to the foot. Probably just too lazy, or didn't have a hammer and nails lying around. I was thinking too much.

I pulled at the wood and climbed through the house, grocery bag first, followed by an entering that would have made the most skilled burglar proud. If there was any sound made at all it was by the wind, not by me. I picked up the groceries and walked up the stairs, slowly. As my eyes made it past the floor and into the room ahead, I saw the room was empty. No cardboard bed. No cardboard nightstand. He must have gotten spooked and ditched this house for another.

I decided to search the upstairs anyway and took another step up, when something hit my shoulder. I ducked and swung my arm out but by then it had wrapped around my neck and tightened. The junkie stood over the railing above me, holding tight to a rope; the other end formed into a slipknot that now gripped my neck.

"I've had it with you kids, prowling around my business, stealing my things. This ends now, bitch."

I dropped the groceries and reached for the rope that had now gone taut to the point of nearly lifting me off the stairs. I obtained a quick grip on the rope and pulled. The man pulled back. We were in a game of tug-of-war, my neck the center of it all. I couldn't tell what hurt more, the crushing of my throat or the rope sawing through my neck. I thought of trying to jump and climb the rope to him, but if he let go I'd crash down the hard wooden stairs. Instead, I decided to yank again, hold tight and run up the remaining stairs, around the railing and toward the man, giving myself slack and the man a beating.

I did just that, yanked, held tight, and ran. But as I rounded the corner, the man let go of the rope, threw his hands up and screamed "Not in front of Daisy!"

I stopped, then loosened the rope around my neck and dropped it to the ground. Whoever Daisy was she was now in hiding and nowhere to be seen. The man looked terrified, but not of me, of something else.

"Thank you," he said. "Now just leave. *Please*."

There was desperation in his voice that was somehow calming, made me forget that he'd just tried to kill me. I couldn't help but pity him. I held my hands up with my palms open as a symbol of peace and said, "I brought you something."

He gave me a puzzled look and told me he didn't want anything I had. He then backed up, and when he did he limped, favoring his right leg. His ankle was a bulbous mess with dark shades of purple and red.

"The bag I was carrying, it was full of food for you...and heroin. I got it downtown."

He got suspicious and again urged me to leave. I could tell he didn't believe nor trust me. I didn't blame him, but still, the guy was a junkie. They did everything they could to get their hands on the stuff, from turning tricks to stealing from friends and family, but here he was turning away a stranger.

"Kat sent you, didn't he?"

"No. I'm here on my own."

"That makes no sense. I don't even know you. Why would you bring me anything?" His face then gave a look of revelation. "You got some of that bad stuff that's going around...that Rainbow Bright. You're trying to kill me."

I thought it would all go much smoother than it was. I anticipated the junkie clawing his way to his fix, asking questions later, if any at all. As pathetic as the guy's life was, he didn't want to lose it. He had reservations I wasn't expecting. I gained a small amount of respect for him that wasn't there before. A small amount. I decided to tell him of my plan and my reasoning behind it. He listened, with skeptic's ears. I told him about my curiosities, that it would be my first time. When I was done he told me I was nuts, that nobody would ever do what I'm doing. He was convinced I was there to poison him and asked how I knew about him. I said that someone had told me an addict was living out here. It wasn't really a lie, but I didn't let on that I was here just yesterday.

The man stood silent for a moment, thinking, then pointed his finger at me and asked, "Were you one of those punks who was here yesterday? Bashed my ankle?"

I lied and told him it wasn't me, then looked at his ankle and acted surprised, told him it looked like it hurt. I said I was going downstairs to gather everything I dropped and that I'd be right back. I picked up the rope and took it with me. He stood over the railing and watched me. When gathering the food I put it all back in the bag but slipped the zippered pouch down the front of my pants.

"Is that a honey bun?"

"It is. You okay with that?" He didn't answer. He walked around the railing and met me at the top of the stairs, reaching out for the bag. I hesitated before handing it to him. "We got a deal then? You gonna help me do this?"

The man nodded, snatched the bag from me and said, "You're shootin' first. And I ain't using a needle after you so I hope you brought your own."

I told him I did, that I brought everything I thought we needed. I followed him down the hall and into a room where he'd moved his "furniture." The room was similar in size to the other and he'd set it up just like the last one, though in here cardboard hung nailed over the windows acting as curtains. I took note there was no sign of anyone else. I asked him about Daisy. He told me not to worry about her, that I'd meet her later. If I turned out cool.

We sat across from each other, him on the cardboard bed and me on the floor against the wall. He dumped the contents of the bag onto the floor and picked through it.

"Some of this is for you, ain't it?"

"Yes. Unless you're really that hungry, then you can have it all."

"Here, you'd better at least take this." He tossed me one of the cans of coke and a granola bar. "You'll probably be puking, and you don't want to be dry heaving. It's worse."

"Okay, thanks." I opened the granola bar and took a bite.

"I don't see the goods here, man. What gives?"

I pulled the pouch out of my pants and opened it, took out one of the balloons and tossed it to the man.

"Aww, shit. You got tar. I'm not shooting this."

"What's wrong with that?" I asked.

"A couple things. I can tell you right now this came from Chaz. You said you got this downtown, right?

"Yeah, Hillcrest."

"Near Van Buren?"

"Yeah, at the corner of Washington.

"Yeah, that's Chaz. This stuff isn't even *half* pure. Plus tar ain't good for your veins."

"I don't think any of it is."

"Yeah, but tar is worse. You see my toes?" The man held up one of his feet and showed me the stump where his big toe had been. "I used to shoot in my toes when I first started. Tried hiding the habit. I only shot tar then. My toes rotted, stunk for weeks until I had to have them cut off."

"Damn!"

"Yeah. Well, I'm diabetic too so that might have something to do with it." He took a bite of the honey bun.

"How do you get your insulin?" I asked.

"I don't. It's diet controlled. Go figure."

"So I wasted my money on this?"

"Nah, we'll chase it."

"Chase it?"

"We'll smoke it. I got everything we need. Man, I haven't had a honey bun since probably high school. Used to eat them every day back then."

I was a little disappointed. I didn't even know you could smoke heroin, and injecting it was what I'd had my mind set on. It's the demon I wanted to stare at face to face. I'd smoked before—pot. But never injected anything. The tar didn't seem like much of a challenge, and I wasn't sure I'd have the same high people couldn't seem to let go of.

"Can you smoke it and I shoot it?" I asked.

"Listen, man. If you wanna get high like you said, then Chaz's junk isn't the way to go. You'll get high, sure, but not *high*, high. If you're gonna throw your life away you may as well do it right. 'Cuz you ain't gonna turn out the chipper you think you are."

"Do you have any we could shoot?"

"Sure don't, so you made good timing. Would have been a miserable day without ya."

The guy took his orange tray and a triangular wooden box I hadn't seen before and set it on the cardboard bed. The box was one of those military things you see at a veteran's memorial—glass top, holds an American flag inside all folded up nice and neat. I couldn't see what was inside the box but he pulled out a lighter, a thick plastic straw that looked like an empty pen, and a small jack knife.

"Down that coke."

"I will."

"I mean now, man. We need the tin if we're gonna do this."

44

It was all happening so fast now. Only minutes ago I was climbing through the window with a bag of junk food, and here we are getting ready to prep the drug so many chased after and even more ran from. The guy eating the honey bun was a completely different person than the one who was afraid I'd poison him. Now he was ready. The food had been a better offering than I'd thought.

I popped the lid on the coke and drank as much as I could, washing down the rest of the granola bar. I was getting nervous and stalled a bit. "What's your name?" I asked the man.

"My name's, Dave. Yours?"

"Chris."

"Chris Piss...you get that a lot?"

"Not really. First I've heard it."

"I'd call you Chris Piss if you were my friend." He took the last bite of his honey bun and wiped his hands on his shorts. "Let me hit that." He reached his hand out for the coke. I gave it to him and asked him how long he's lived here.

"Don't know. If I had to guess I'd say two months tops. I don't stick around the same place too long." He downed the rest of the coke and took his knife and poked a hole in the can, doing his best to slice it, then pulled a wide strip down from the top, making a metal scoop with it. "I got no foil but this'll do."

He took the heroin out of one of the balloons, pinched off a small piece and set it on the tin lip he'd formed, then pulled the tab up at the top and held it like a lantern.

"Take the tooter." He nodded toward the tray. "And inhale all the smoke through it once you see it rising."

My heart raced and my palms felt clammy. As I reached for the straw, my hand shook. He could see it. He was watching me.

"I'm telling you right now, man, you're gonna get sick. But you're not dying, so don't worry. Chaz's tar ain't nothin' you can't handle."

I grabbed the straw.

"Let's get it on," Dave said as he sparked a flame under the tin lip. "Keep your eye on it."

I watched the black blob as it settled in the fold of the tin, then put the straw in my mouth and leaned toward the can, wondering what inside that little globule turned people into slaves, giving up so much. Their dignity.

Esteem. Integrity. Money. Mental and physical health. Friends and family. Shelter. Morals. Opportunity. Dreams and goals. After a while, I saw smoke but didn't inhale. I froze. I was lost in thought being so close to the bubbling demon.

"Hit it, man!" Dave's voice startled me and I drew in as much of the smoke as I could. It hit my tongue like sea salt and tasted of burnt ham cooked in vinegar. My throat burned, the smoke more harsh than any tobacco or marijuana I'd ever had. I tried my hardest not to cough but it didn't work. I turned my head away from Dave and let go, the acidic vinegar taste coating my tongue one last time as it exited in a small cloud before me. The coughing fit I experienced next I swear used every muscle in my body. Although my throat burned as though I'd swallowed tacks, the rest of my body tingled. The muscles that had tensed through the fit now relaxed, and any anxiety I'd felt before was gone. I leaned back to my spot against the wall and waited. Slowly, over the next several minutes, a warmth that felt like dipping into a tub of heated oil came over me.

"That's it?" Dave said. "There's plenty more here, boy. You're gonna want at least a few more hits." Dave then took the straw from me, lit his lighter and readied himself for a hit. He exhaled to the point of making some strange noise in his chest, then inhaled through the straw like he was fresh out of the water and hungry for air. He didn't cough. He held his hit in, holding his breath for as long as he could. When he finally did exhale there was barely a sign of any smoke.

"That's how it's done." He came toward me with the butchered coke can, handing me the straw. He held the flame under the lip, and I waited for the smoke. This time I exhaled, then inhaled much like Dave had done. The coughing was less of a fit this time, and though I'd taken a bigger hit, there was less smoke than before. And as a result I was much higher than I had been. The tingling in my body increased, as did the calm. The euphoria. I sat back against the wall completely content. Dave scooted back to his cardboard bed and finished off the rest of the tar that lie melting in the can. He then added more and finished that off too.

Finally, Dave leaned back and asked me how I felt. I told him I felt good, real good. He smiled and told me my life was over and that he hopes I enjoyed the eighteen or nineteen years I've had. Had I not been high, I suppose the declaration may have bothered me, but I wasn't about to listen to some vagrant junkie tell me I'd lost control because of one date with the drug.

Only minutes went by before Dave loaded up the coke can and began smoking again. He didn't seem to be having as much fun as I was. He itched himself quite a bit and then I started itching. I took notice that part of the wall behind him was adorned with the same flowers as the other room. Soon after my discovery, I watched Dave as he put down the can and started drawing more tiny flowers to join the others on the wall.

"You're an artist?" I asked him.

"Not really. I've never drawn a thing in my life until a few years ago."

"You really like flowers, huh?"

He didn't answer me, just held his tongue out while he drew, like a child; every bit of attention on each tiny flower. At the time, it was a beautiful sight to see someone so lost and dedicated, but later it bothered me a bit. While he drew he'd shift around clumsily to get comfortable on the cardboard, being careful to avoid putting any weight on his ankle. I felt bad about what had happened and nearly told him right then that it was my friend who'd hit him. But as good as I felt in that moment, like nothing could ever go wrong, I was able to hold my tongue.

"Why are you drawing flowers all over the house?"

"They're not for me."

"Who are they for?"

Again, he didn't answer. Instead he grabbed the can, loaded it and smoked more. He asked me if I wanted more and I did. I wasn't coming down yet so I'm not sure why I continued. I guess because it felt like the right thing to do. Everything was perfect in that moment and trying to go beyond that sounded appealing. And possible.

After he picked the pencil back up I asked him again who the flowers were for. He said they were for Daisy. I'd forgotten about her and asked him where she was.

"She left."

"Is she coming back?"

"No. Maybe tomorrow."

"Is she your girlfriend?"

Dave stopped drawing and stared at me and asked if I was going to gab all day or sit back and cuddle with God. I think four hours went by sitting there, smoking the rest of the tar. And other than Dave rambling about his favorite music, films, and books, and then asking me mine, there wasn't much talk between us. At one point I dozed off and fell asleep for at least a few hours. When I woke again my neck hurt from slouching, and from the rope. But other than that I felt fine–better than I'd expected, actually. I needed to get the car back to Dad so I told Dave I was leaving. And in a moment that can only be described as awkward, I thanked him.

"Don't thank me, man. All you did was sell your soul for a dirty black bean. You may think you saw God, but that was a decoy. That garbage Chaz pawns off as heroin ain't nothing but baby food. I drink straight from the teat. The junk I get blows your mind, runs through your body like liquid gold...a great 'gasm to behold."

"I dunno, man. It felt pretty good to me."

"Baby food fills a baby, don't it?"

Dave certainly had a way with words. I said goodbye and he said he'd see me soon. I'm not sure why he said that, but I was very adamant about this being a one-time thing. I knew I was done here and I left Limewood feeling confident that my curiosity had been quelled. I now knew what heroin felt like. And surprisingly there didn't seem to be any repercussions, except a small headache. No bad hangover. No coming down. And I hadn't even gotten sick like Dave said. Most importantly, as I drove home I had no irresistible urge for more. I was a free man.

3: Denial

That night Eddie and Kent called and asked if I wanted to hang out, but I stayed at home. Being around those two didn't sound appealing anymore. All I had on my mind was what I'd just been through at Limewood. And no way was I telling them about it.

I spent most of the night reading *Trout Fishing in America* by Richard Brautigan. Somehow I thought it'd help me understand Dave a bit more. It didn't. If anything, it confused me all the more. I didn't get the book at all, so I stopped about halfway through it.

I thought a lot about what Dave had said about the heroin we'd had and how I didn't *really* follow through with my initial plan, to take it intravenously. I could tell right away it wasn't a problem and couldn't find any reason not to try it one more time. For real this time, using Dave's source. I decided I'd head out the next day and see if Dave was up for a drive, then that would be it. I would try it for real and then be done. And nobody would ever know I'd dabbled. The secret was mine and Dave's. And Daisy's if she was there.

***

I waited until after I'd eaten lunch this time, then went to Limewood using Dad's car. I told him I had an interview and if I didn't get the job that I was heading to a job fair down at the college and maybe fill out some more apps on the way home. I took the pouch with the needles, lighter, spoon and cotton balls and put it in a backpack, along with some snacks, coke, and my dad's copy of *Trout Fishing in America*–another peace offering for Dave. Dad wouldn't notice it was gone. The books on his shelf all held decades of dust, just stuff from the 60s and 70s that he couldn't seem to let go of.

This time when I climbed through Dave's window I announced myself. He asked if I was alone and then yelled to come on up. As I walked through the house I could smell the bucket he'd kept in the closet, mostly the urine. It reminded me of the bathroom at the beach one year. Both toilets were broken but no turds were in sight, just the darkest urine you'd ever seen, like a dark German beer. I'd learned in health class that dark, foul-smelling urine could be the sign of a health issue. But I suppose pissing in the same bucket for weeks would tend to darken and smell despite your health.

When I got upstairs to Dave's room he was flipping through the pages of the flower book. He didn't look up, didn't say a word, so I watched him for a minute. It was a bit awkward. I mean, this wasn't a friend of mine. He was a deteriorating junkie, and I was a kid fresh out of high school with the world by the balls. Yesterday had been like a bad one-night stand that was dangerous for the both of us. We both knew better but never acknowledged the sin.

Finally, I spoke up. "Studying flowers?"

"I smoked it all, kid."

"That's fine. I don't want it anyway. I wanna shoot up. I want to get the stuff you were talking about, from your source."

Dave looked up from the book, squinted at me. "I'm out. And I wouldn't share it with you anyway." He saw I was holding a backpack. "You bring more food?"

"I did." I took off the backpack and started pulling out the food. "Sorry, I didn't bring any honey buns, but I got some chips, more granola bars, and these." I handed Dave a box of Nilla Wafers.

"I'm a heroin junkie, not a junk food junkie. I told you about the diabetes, right?"

"Sorry, man. I don't have a job. I grabbed all this from home."

"Your mom don't cook?"

"Yeah, but I tried to grab stuff that didn't need refrigerating."

"You're over thinking it, man. I haven't had a home-cooked meal in....well, in a damn long time."

"Here, I brought this for you, too." I handed him the copy of *Trout Fishing in America*.

Dave kind of smiled, sideways like. "Brautigan...you read?"

"Not much. I did read some of that last night, though."

"Great, ain't it?"

I didn't really want to get into my honest thoughts on the book. I just wanted Dave to get in the car, take a drive, and score some of this magic heroin he was talking about so I could be on my way, so I just told him I hadn't finished it yet. He took the book and set it along with the others, then tidied them into a little stack, like he was proud of his growing collection. His smile went full.

"So you've got no money for some H?" Dave asked.

"No, I've got money for that."

"Just not for food." He said it like I was an idiot. And for one quick moment I felt like a kid being reprimanded by his disappointed father. But this was a homeless junkie who tossed his morals out long ago, someone with no right to talk down to me. I wasn't like him. I was better than him.

"Listen, man. I brought money for you and me to get some heroin, and I've got a ride parked outside behind the house, so if you want to show off that liquid gold then let's go do it, otherwise I'll do it myself."

I think Dave realized the situation because he set the book down and stood up as fast as his swollen ankle would allow and said: "Let's go."

***

Dave had me head out to Mustang, an island across the bridge by the gulf. It was mostly upper class and certainly not an area you'd run into people like Dave. He had me stop two blocks from a street that led into a subdivision, then he walked on his own the rest of the way and disappeared around the corner. It was hard watching him walk with a limp, knowing Eddie had done that. Dave certainly didn't deserve it. At least not from what I'd seen.

I sat and waited for Dave while The Rolling Stones played on about how it's all right, in fact it's a gas. The song ended and Dave still wasn't back. I half expected him to be chased out of the subdivision by a group of middle-aged men with a beer in one hand and a golf club in the other, sporting plaid shorts and lawn-stained loafers. But regardless of why we were there, I almost felt safe in the neighborhood. A far cry from the dreary, rundown ghetto that is Hillcrest. Before the next song ended, Dave came around the corner up ahead, limping speedily toward me. He must have heard me start the car because he put his hand up as though telling me to stay there.

Once in the car, Dave told me that I didn't want to get involved with people like this and the less they know about me and what I'm driving, the better. I agreed, even if this was a one-time thing.

On the way back to Limewood, there was silence between us. Again it was awkward, and I can't really compare it to anything except maybe what it would feel like to be in the car with a prostitute. You're both about to do something immoral and degrading, a low you both never thought you'd sink to and you'd rather not talk about it. But I think the silence was almost worse. At least for me it was. Maybe Dave just didn't care. Maybe he was past that point, and nobody meant anything to him. I was just an opportunity to get high and he'd given up on himself long ago.

We made our way through the house and into the room before Dave broke the silence. He told me I would shoot first, then he would. He asked me if I'd eaten and I told him I had. He said he thinks I didn't get sick before because of Chaz's bogus supply but this time I most likely would so not to sit next to him. I started to tell him, again, that I thought the black tar was good stuff but kept my mouth shut.

I gave Dave the zippered pouch and told him everything we needed was in there. He emptied the pouch and said, "No water? No tie off?" He reached behind his nightstand box and grabbed a bottle of tap water that was only half full. I got nervous, not knowing if there was any way I could get AIDS or hepatitis from the water. I thought I'd been so careful to bring everything we needed, with it all being sterile. I was too scared to ask Dave if I was in any danger from the water. I didn't want to insult him. I convinced myself that if there was anything to catch that it would be from a needle, not from bottled water.

I watched Dave as he took the small envelope of heroin he bought and poured some into the spoon, the spoon being propped up onto one of the books he'd now set on the cardboard bed. It was strange seeing my mother's silverware being used as paraphernalia for shooting heroin. I've eaten with that silverware my whole life. Shit, my mother probably fed me with it before I could even hold it myself.

Before I bummed myself out, Dave broke my gaze on the spoon by tossing a shoelace at me, telling me to wrap it around my arm a few times just under my armpit, tighten it, and hold it there. He said my veins were healthy and we'd have no problem, that they'd suck the H up like a sponge.

Dave mixed the heroin with water and stirred it with the plunger end of the syringe, mashing down any powder that had yet to dissolve. He then lit the small candle he had on his box nightstand and held the spoon over it, letting the flame lick the underside until the liquid inside bubbled. He quickly set it back down and uncapped the syringe.

As he was about to lay the needle in the spoon, I asked him about using the cotton first. He said: "We don't need it. I'm telling you, this is the purest junk you're ever gonna find."

He laid the needle into the liquid and slowly sucked the contents up into the syringe, then held the needle up and pushed the plunger, causing any air to exit. The whole process was done with almost muscle memory maneuvers, in a way only a veteran could do.

"You're up," Dave said as he scooted toward me with needle in hand. I wasn't quite as nervous as I had been the day before. I knew more of what to expect. Or thought I did.

I expected Dave to massage my arm like they do in the movies, but he didn't need to. My veins were bulging, waiting. Dave held my arm, and with precision that could only be topped by the most skilled nurse, slid the needle into my arm, then pulled at the plunger and I saw my blood mix with the heroin. He told me to loosen the shoelace and then slowly injected the syringe's contents into me. My body slouched against the wall, and that rush through my body, though similar to yesterday, intensified into something completely different. Something I'm not sure I have the words for, as though the very clouds themselves picked me up and held me closer to the glow of the sun, gently massaging me. It was hard to picture the high being any better than it was yesterday, but Dave was right. Here I was, floating in an invisible warm gel with not a care in the world, resting comfortably in the deepest recesses of my own mind.

Until I vomited.

It just came up, unexpectedly. The nausea was an afterthought, and though my stomach suddenly seemed to disagree with my current state, it still didn't seem to matter. I was content. I wiped my face with the back of my hand and sat there against the wall in my own puke as though it had been nothing more than spray from a sneeze.

I could hear Dave tell me I'd be cleaning that up, but I was in my own world, living out vivid daydreams. Some were nostalgic where I visited my grandmother's house in Springfield, sitting on her back porch where we would watch birds while eating popcorn and drinking ginger ale, her flower garden before us filled with hummingbirds, frogs, and squirrels. Another moment was completely fictional where I was living in California, walking down Sunset Boulevard, the sun paving my way as people on the sidewalks cheered me on, taking my picture, asking for my autograph, and kissing me. Everyone loved me, and I loved myself, was proud of myself for my accomplishments.

I could hear Dave taking care of the needles and the spoon and water, all of it. He was a real neat freak, even when high. Most the time he wouldn't even kick back until everything was in its place. He didn't like being disorganized.

Then I heard Dave say something about how Daisy is coming, and for a moment I was embarrassed that she'd see me this way but then knew she'd understand, so I looked forward to it. I opened my eyes—or maybe they were already open—and looked at Dave who had just pulled the needle from his arm, sitting back on his stack of cardboard. He was looking toward the doorway and there was a smile on his face. He mouthed something but I couldn't make it out. He was speaking so softly I couldn't tell if he was only mouthing the words or I was just too high to hear him.

Finally, I heard him say "I love you, Daisy." I looked around the room but saw no one. She was in the hallway, out of my line of sight. Dave tilted his head, and the look on his face was of both sorrow and gratitude. A tear ran down his face and was eaten by his scruff. I couldn't tell if he was sad or in a euphoric state of pure joy. Then he closed his eyes and grimaced with an equally confusing look of either pleasure or pain.

Dave then grabbed a pencil and started drawing flowers while talking to Daisy, who at this point still hadn't entered the room.

"Some kids came in while I was sleeping. Don't think it's broke, though." Dave said. "No, it'll be fine. Just need to stay off from it for a while. It looks worse than it is. Don't you worry."

As his conversation with Daisy went on, I still couldn't hear her. Had I been on pot it probably would have freaked me out. But instead, I imagined the two speaking telepathically and deemed it a beautiful form of communication between two lovers. If that's what they were, lovers. He never told me.

I kind of drifted in and out of these daydreams–more fantasies under the California sun, time with Grandmother. I couldn't tell which ones were memories long forgotten or things I'd made up. Nevertheless, each one was worth reveling in, if even while leaned against an unfinished townhome wall, a homeless man across from me obsessively drawing tiny flowers for no apparent reason.

I realized just how hot I was, like being cooked alive. I took off my shirt, which took some doing. It came in stages. First one arm out, pause. Then another, pause. Then over my head, where I kept it on like a mask for several minutes, lost in my high. Periodically I would itch. I pictured my skin rippling like water each time I scratched it. Warm water.

"His name is Chris."

I was alerted by my name being said, but not enough to peek around and through the doorway to see Dave's friend-lover.

"I'm keeping him safe, but he's killed himself. He's a corpse now."

Dave kept on talking but I paid no attention, and Daisy never came into the room.

After what I guess would have been the pinnacle of my high, I watched Dave draw his flowers. It was relaxing, but impossible to picture myself doing much of anything other than sitting perfectly still. No doubt Dave had a high tolerance. Perhaps drawing enhanced his own high, helped him forget, to get lost within himself. I remember a friend of mine once drew a bird's eye view of a small city on the tile floor of his bathroom while stoned and on the toilet. Buildings, cars driving down streets, pedestrians. All in different colored markers. Dave reminded me of that. But this was much more than envisioning something on a tile floor while shitting. This was pure obsession. Dave's compulsion to draw the flowers would lead to my preoccupation with needing to know why.

As my high wound down, I grew tired and hungry so I ate some of the food I'd brought. Without putting too much thought into it, I blurted out the words: "It was me and my friends who broke in here and woke you up. My friend Eddie hit you with a tire iron."

Dave stopped drawing and stared deep into his lead perennial garden. I wasn't entirely convinced he would hear me. But he had.

"I didn't touch you, though. Or any of your stuff. It was Eddie. I didn't think it was cool. I'm sorry."

Dave continued to glare at the wall, never looking at me. "I know. Daisy saw you." Then went back to drawing.

I'm not sure, but I think the hair on my arms rose. I doubted Daisy's existence anymore. I hadn't seen her, hadn't heard her, and now I was supposed to believe she was watching us while my friends and I were here. I sat up and crawled to the doorway, looked

67

out and down the hall. Nothing. No one was there.

"There is no Daisy. You're messing with me."

Dave stopped drawing again. This time he looked at me, rage in his eyes. "She left. She was standing right there, you asshole! Save your paranoia for the weed."

Dave was convincing. I heavily considered that maybe I was too high. It made perfect sense to have my blood filled with the drug and miss out on things around me, I guess. Especially when it's my first time. And I suppose it was possible that Daisy had been in another room, hiding from us when we were here before. We didn't check all the rooms. As a matter of fact, except for the laundry room, kitchen and living room, we didn't look anywhere.

I told Dave I was sorry. He didn't seem to care and went back to drawing. And because this was to be a one-time adventure with the heroin—excluding the black tar, that didn't count—I spent the rest of the time keeping to myself and taking it all in, every moment.

Unfortunately, it didn't last nearly as long as I had hoped. And by the time I came down,

I didn't feel good. I was nauseous, my head was pounding, and my legs were weak.

I cleaned up the puke as much as I could, using my shirt as a rag to wipe up the floor. It was a bit difficult without running water. I told Dave that the Brautigan book was a gift and that he could keep it—even though he'd already added it to his small collection—as well as the rest of the food. I told him one more time that I was sorry about his ankle. He said not to worry about it and then said if my friends ever showed their face here again he'd stick them with every needle he had. Then, just like last time, he said he'd see me soon. The words cramped my stomach and haunted me for the next few days.

4: Delusions

Over the next few days I continued to keep my distance from Eddie and Kent. We'd become different people. Eddie was a cruel bully and Kent was just a pussy along for the ride. My experience with Dave allowed for some empathy I'd never had before–sympathy for his situation. I'd seen a human side to him rather than the waste of space I admit to viewing him as before. In general, I started to look at people differently. Every one of us has our demons and we're all scared of something, running from something. Hiding something.

I couldn't stop thinking about Daisy and how I hadn't met her. And the more I thought of it, the more I thought Dave was out of his mind and hallucinating, talking to himself like those guys I see walking down Fremont Street near the adult foster care homes. After three long days, I needed to know. I headed back to Limewood with Dad's car once again, food in hand. This time I had no money left of my own so I took several rolls of quarters my dad kept in a jar on his dresser, forty dollars worth. I also took a few clean needles. I thought maybe Dave could use them. I'd just leave them with him. I was only going there to meet Daisy. I knew he may want a ride to score, and I was okay with that. But this time it was all about Daisy.

It's what I told myself anyway, right up until I had the needle in my arm a second time.

When I showed up at Limewood, Dave shook his head when he saw me. He seemed to have mixed feelings about me being there–disappointed in me but grateful for the company. I think I understood. We scored some H and went back to Limewood where we prepped and booted up.

This time I made sure to sit next to Dave in front of the doorway. While he was helping tie me off, I asked him about Daisy. I asked if she was going to come around, told him I'd really like to meet her. He said that she'd be here and he felt good about me meeting her. I asked where she slept, then he stuck me with the needle and I didn't care anymore.

After Dave shot, he sat still for a few minutes, taking in the rush, then went to drawing. The care he took on each petal of each flower was impressive. From where I sat I could see intricate details I hadn't noticed before. He whispered quietly as he drew. Between the quiet of his voice and the gentle motion of his hand, I fell under a heavy daze, lost in the collage of flowers being birthed.

"Hey, honey." Dave's voice startled me. My eyes had closed at some point, but I felt like I was still watching him. I looked at the doorway but no one was there. I looked around the room. Nothing.

"Don't be afraid, Daisy." Dave pleaded.

There was no one there. I made a bold move and confronted Dave.

"There's nobody there, man. We're alone."

"Can you see her now? She's crying, bro. She doesn't wanna be here."

There was no one there. I wondered if this was mental illness or the drugs. Or worse yet, mental illness caused by the very drugs that now ran through my veins. He kept on about Daisy and how she was there and I should be able to see her and that maybe it's because I'm not empathetic, maybe I don't care about other people suffering. But that wasn't true. I cared now. I hated people like Eddie and Kent—bullies and pussies.

"She's losing her teeth." He said finally. "She's pissing her pants, the poor girl."

His words were sobering. I became frightened. I wasn't sure how to react. Do I humor him and pretend that I saw her? Or ignore him and hope his episode passed soon? I decided that ignoring was best and so I sat there, trying to enjoy my high while he sobbed, whispering "I'm sorry" over and over again. Eventually he stopped, said "Don't worry, you'll never be like this" and went back to drawing the flowers.

Later we found ourselves in civil conversation. It turns out Dave had gone to school at one point and majored in business administration but dropped out after his second year and joined the military instead. Less than a year later he'd been discharged but didn't say why. He said it was for the best and that he never should have signed up in the first place, that he should have finished school and made something of himself.

While we talked, I started to smell the bucket of waste from downstairs. The upstairs used to be safe from the reek but not anymore. It was getting stronger. I asked him about it and told him he should go dump it somewhere, bury it even. He told me he couldn't smell it and then changed the subject.

I ended up crashing there that night. It was horribly uncomfortable on the wooden floor. When I first fell asleep I didn't mind either way, but after a few hours I woke up and shifted restlessly the remainder of the night. When I got up in the morning Dave was already awake. He was reading *Trout Fishing in America* and sipping on gas station coffee.

"Where'd you get that?" I asked him.

"Store down the road. Older lady, Marjorie, works mornings there. Always hooks me up." He pointed to the box nightstand. "Got you one too."

There on the box sat a steaming, lidded white cup that read "Crystal Flash Gas & Go" on the side.

"Thanks." I grabbed the cup and took a sip. I normally didn't drink coffee but somehow that morning it felt right. I looked out the window. Everything was wet. It must have rained while we slept. We don't get enough of it, and I was sorry I'd missed it.

"You like the book?" I asked Dave.

"I do, thanks."

I told him I thought the book was bizarre and that after I had read a few of the chapters I still didn't get it. He laughed and said that I was thinking too hard, that there's really nothing to get. That I should just appreciate the odd bits of Brautigan's brain that he shared with us while he was alive.

"I got these, too." Dave reached into a bag and pulled out two hotdogs and a few packages of ketchup. "They throw them out after a day." He handed the hot dogs and ketchup to me. There was no bun, just the meat, pruned like a raisin from sitting under a heat lamp for too many hours the day before.

I drank the coffee and ate the dogs and thought about my dad and how pissed he must be that I wasn't home yet with his car. I didn't care. I'd be moving out soon and wouldn't have to deal with him or his rules or his lying, cheating ass.

I took my time with the rest of the coffee while Dave read a passage he thought was funny. It was, when taken out of context. One thing's for sure. Richard Brautigan really liked trout. Or symbolism. Or drugs.

I wanted to bring up Daisy but I didn't. I knew Dave wouldn't have any clear answer for me and I didn't want to put him on the spot, maybe stir up some unnecessary agitation. Things seemed pretty cool between the two of us now and I wanted it to stay that way. You'd think there wouldn't be much to respect about Dave, but there was. And I'm not sure why. He'd given up on himself and any goal he may have once had, but somehow I was able to look past that.

Empathy.

I told Dave I needed to get going and thanked him for breakfast. He nodded, and the words "I'll see you soon" slipped out of my mouth.

5: Headfirst

I was right. Dad was furious. He said I was
grounded from the car for a month and that
I'd be lucky if I ever got to use it again. Mom
seemed pretty disappointed in me but stayed
out of it. She usually did. In the past four
years I can count on two hands how many
hours Mom had spent interacting with me.
Four years. And that was just small talk in the
car when she'd give me rides to school.
Apparently for her, parenting stopped around
the time my puberty kicked in.

***

Later that night I felt uneasy and antsy,
shaky even. I told myself it was stress. I'd
been through a lot lately, plus I hadn't been
eating well. I decided that living at home
wasn't for me anymore, that I'd had enough
of my parents. I filled my backpack with a
few changes of clothes and as many snacks as
I could find—I even grabbed a loaf of bread
and some peanut butter. I also took two more
needles from Dad and every roll of quarters
he had. He'd notice them gone this time. It
was scary how little I cared.

I saw my cell phone sitting on my dresser. It was covered in a thin layer of dust. I hadn't had service since I'd turned eighteen—my dad's idea of giving me incentive to get a job, said he'd no longer pay for the service. So there it sat. I wasn't one of these people who really got off on staring at that little screen, playing games, looking at other people's lives. Little did my dad know I actually enjoyed not having the thing stuck to me all the time. I mean, who wants to never be able to get away from people, especially their parents?

By 10:00 p.m. I was on the road and heading to the closest bus stop on foot. The nearest bus route took me about a mile from Limewood so I walked the rest of the way. On the way there, as though God himself was providing, I found a mattress lying off the freeway in the ditch. It was one of those small vinyl ones you stick in a baby's crib, but it sure beat wood or cardboard. I figured it fell off a truck during someone's move. I picked it up and carried it the rest of the way to Limewood. I think it was even lighter than the backpack strapped to me.

It was after midnight by the time I got to Dave's. He was thankful that I'd brought him the mattress but said he liked the cardboard bed and that I could sleep on the mattress if I wanted. That's the moment I realized I wasn't going anywhere—something I think he'd known all along.

I asked him if it was too late to score and he said if we wanted the good junk then it was definitely too late, but if we wanted to head downtown and get something else then no hour was too late, so that's where we headed, via bus. On the way there, Dave shared with me how he'd get his food. Most of it he ate from dumpsters. He said there were a few stores that threw away perfectly good food. He said he'd hit the dumpsters a few days a week and come home with at least two or three days worth, plus there was Marjorie at Crystal Flash.

I asked him about showering and clean clothes. He said he had two sets of clothes, one he'd wear while washing the other in the bathroom sink at Crystal Flash, then bring them home to dry. He'd use the same sink to wash up and shave. He said he kept a razor, toothbrush and paste, and a bar of soap hidden in a Ziploc bag in one of the toilet tanks so he didn't have to carry it around with him. It grossed me out at first but then I thought it was rather resourceful, ingenious even.

By the time we got back to Limewood it was nearly 2:00 a.m. I was tired and wondered if waiting until tomorrow would make more sense, but it was clear Dave didn't think so, and so we shot up and enjoyed the rest of the night.

Until Dave thought Daisy was there.

He didn't start crying like he did last time. He mostly just smiled and whispered, said the occasional sentence that I could never make out. I just let him be. It was clear by now that Dave had another side to him that was unhealthy, and because I didn't know his history I felt it was best to leave it alone. Who was I to try and convince him things did or did not exist.

***

For the next few days Dave and I made trips to Mustang and scored some of the good junk. It would have been nice to get more in one run but the guy wouldn't sell like that. He told Dave that he never kept much on him, that it was delivered each day. Sounded like horseshit to me. I think the guy was afraid of being robbed, that the wrong people would find out he's got crates full of liquid gold in there worth millions, or something.

Dave talked a lot about getting a car one day. It was just wishful thinking. Any money we got went right into our veins. I think he'd just talk about it because we both hated to walk and it's what kept him going, maybe he thought it's what kept me going with him.

I started keeping my own personal hygiene bag in one of the toilets along with Dave's. It was nice to be able to brush my teeth nearly every day. I was sure that eventually someone would find those bags and throw them out, but they never did.

6: Consequences

It took an entire week of staying at Limewood for me to admit to myself that I'd let the drug take me. And I hated myself for it. Up until then I'd made excuses: My parents don't love me. I'm just a teenager celebrating graduation, living life a little before adulthood. They were all lies and I knew it. I had let heroin become my master. Any delusions I had about being stronger than I really was were gone. And though life was bleak, I had hope that I wouldn't always be like this, that one day I'd make a stand against the drug and walk away. Just not yet.

***

Another three weeks went by with Dave and me feeding our addiction. It had gotten bad. We were starting to steal from a few of the stores nearby and even staked out a house along our usual route, eventually breaking in and walking away with a few thousand dollars in cash, a bunch of candles, silverware, jewelry, and a guitar. We had no problem unloading the stuff. The local pawnshop was as crooked as we were. They'd turn around and ship the stuff two hours away to their sister store and sell anything there they suspected as stolen merch.

My arms were already in pretty bad shape. My left arm in particular. I had a few areas where open sores had formed, spots I'd tried injecting the heroin when it wasn't in a vein. Something Dave hadn't warned me about. Of course it didn't help that we'd been using the same dull needles ever since I'd left my parent's house. But I tried keeping my arms as clean as I could. I'd heard about people getting infections, like Dave's toes. I didn't want that to happen to me.

I caught myself in the mirror one day at Crystal Flash. I had several small sores on my face. I was convinced they were bed bug bites from the mattress I'd found. Until Dave told me to stop picking at myself one day while high. It dawned on me I'd been feeling my face for tiny hairs and imperfections, then trying to rid myself of them–anything that didn't feel smooth or natural. Even at eighteen years old I still hadn't grown much facial hair and normally shaved only every week or so, but I started shaving nearly every day so I wouldn't feel the hairs at all.

Sometimes I'd think about Eddie and Kent and wonder if they missed me. They'd never think to look here. I mean, who would? I'd picture them down at Boden's losing money they didn't have. I thought I'd miss them but I didn't. We were different people now. I felt like I'd done a lot of growing up that summer and they hadn't.

I never thought about my parents. They were like a scab that finally healed and now I just ignored the scar left behind, pretended it wasn't there. The only thing I missed about that house was my bed. The crib mattress was small and I took to using a stack of cardboard at the end of it so my legs were level, otherwise I'd wake up cramping.

Dave and I took turns dumping the bucket, burying it all in holes we dug using a shovel we'd found leaning against one of the other townhomes. The chore was a rather disgusting ordeal, our waste fused together in a white bucket splashed several shades of brown with no way of rinsing it. Now that there were two of us living there, I made the suggestion of pissing outside. I'm not sure why Dave hadn't been doing that all along, but it certainly helped with the smell.

Late one night, Dave and I partook for the second time that day. We'd blown all but one of the candles out, as the moon was particularly bright that night and planted a beam right there in the middle of the room— God's spotlight. It was beautiful. The room swirled in oranges and blues and the air smelled of wet earth from a ten-minute downpour we'd had only an hour before.

I had nodded off and was alerted by the sound of gagging, followed by a wet splash. Dave was leaned over his cardboard bed, hovering above a large puddle of vomit, a thick string of saliva connecting him to the floor, glistening under God's spotlight.

I'd never seen Dave get sick before. I asked if he was okay. He never said a word, just puked more; his mouth opening wider than should be allowed. I expected to hear the crack of his jaw as more vomit sprayed, adding to the growing puddle under him.

Making the assumption he was coming down with something, or maybe that day's dumpster food didn't agree with him, I nodded off again, listening to the disturbing noises from across the room, incorporating them into my drug-induced dreams. His retching became the rusty swing on a playground, his pleas for help the sound of a child's laughter. The playground, my favorite place as a child, before mother bored of me.

When I woke, the sun had just begun to brighten the room. The candles now lay flattened in a hardened swirl of unpredictable patterns. And there, where I last saw him, lay Dave. His face buried in yesterday's meal.

Without getting any closer, I could tell he was dead. His face was blackened from the blood settling. The one eye I could see was still open, the ball itself resting in the congealed vomit.

All at once the smell hit me. The vomit, the bulge in the seat of his pants, the dark, unhealthy urine soaked into the very pants he would've had hanging on the clothesline later that day. At first I felt guilty, like I could have done something instead of sit there watching him, then nodding off. But I couldn't have done anything. He didn't choke on his vomit. Moving him would have done nothing. His death had been coming for a long time, chasing after him. I just happened to be in the room when it finally showed up.

I sat and stared at Dave's body for a while, ignoring the smell, contemplating my future. I always thought if either of us was to die from heroin it would be me. Dave was a veteran, knew what he was doing. This was unexpected. I wanted it to be a wakeup call for me, the bottom that would set me back to the straight and narrow where I'd become goal oriented and responsible. But it wasn't. Forcing myself to learn a lesson here was like trying to run underwater. I was going nowhere, I could feel it.

**

I left Dave there in the room and spent the day making food runs. No way was I gonna try and deal with him in the daylight. On the way to Crystal Flash I passed a nice two-story house with a well kempt garden. I took note that it was the third day that week I'd seen the homeowner leave at the same time; must be off to work. If the pattern stayed consistent I'd be giving the inside a once over.

Marjorie at Crystal Flash asked where Dave was. I told her he wasn't feeling well and decided to stay in bed. I picked up two coffees to make it look good. I was a little proud of myself for that one, thinking ahead, especially given the circumstances. My head was in a whole different place with Dave gone. Sadly, one of the first things I thought of was how I had no way of telling which house in Mustang was his source. I'd have to go downtown.

I stayed away from Limewood for the day, thinking, walking, even napping under a group of bushes in someone's side yard. As it grew closer to dark, I headed back to the house to take care of Dave's body and boot up. I was sure there was enough for one fix left in the last batch we scored.

I dug a hole three buildings over, back behind the house. The hole was shallow, no more than three feet deep and by no means evenly rectangular. But it would do—good enough to keep the smell away. I dragged Dave down the stairs and outside, then over to his grave. I wondered if there was anyone out in the world who was missing him, who was holding onto hope that one day he'd show up again clean and sober, to take back the life heroin had stolen from him.

After Dave was in the hole I tried shifting him into a more natural position. It was difficult. He'd sat dead all day, and by now his limbs had made up their mind how they wanted to remain. I started tossing the dirt on Dave, then stopped. I said a few words, something about how I hoped he was in a better place now and that he was a unique soul. I meant every word, but when it came out it sounded disingenuous so I shut my mouth and covered him up. The earth had obvious markings of a grave so I tried scattering the dirt around, making the area wider. It still looked like a grave. I then took a rock and placed it in the dirt as an unmarked tombstone, and as a landmark for me so I'd never dump the shit bucket on Dave.

I tried cleaning up the room as much as I could using Dave's other set of clothes as rags, then dumped them in the bucket where I'd bury them next time I emptied it. The room still stunk, and honestly I didn't feel right sitting in there without Dave. So I gathered up his things: the books, the orange tray with our rigs on it, the paper and the pencils, as well as all the candles and my mattress and moved them in another of the upstairs rooms we'd never used. It was smaller but clean.

When putting the books away I noticed a bookmark sticking out of the illustrated book of flowers. I opened to the saved page. At the top, in bold black letters, it read: *"Bellis perennis: The Daisy."* I could feel my face go pale, my mouth dry. The word was horrifying and sad. I shut the book and neatly stacked it with the others like Dave would have and went straight for the tray. I was right. There was enough H to get off. I prepped and grabbed my needle and made a note to get rid of Dave's needle the next chance I got.

I'd become pretty good at setting up my own rig. I suppose it's sad to boast about such a thing. But what else was there? Stealthy thief? Hasty gravedigger? Heartless eulogy giver? I got myself comfortable before hitting up. I felt like this one was an homage to Dave. It was also the last time I'd be able to get the good junk.

I spent the rest of the evening not caring anymore that Dave was dead.

7: Revelations

To get through the next few weeks, I stole from open garages and hit the usual dumpsters. You'd be surprised what kind of valuables people leave in their garage, the doors wide open. I stayed away from Crystal Flash, never went back. Not even to get my Ziploc. I knew Marjorie would keep asking questions about Dave and I'd run out of things to say. I'm not a very good liar. My dad used to say I had a "tell." I wasn't sure what he meant until I tried playing poker once at Boden's.

I ended up heading downtown for all my H. It wasn't as good, but there was no way I was about to head out to Mustang, start knocking on doors, asking random people if this is where the good junk is. I'd buy in bigger quantities than Dave and I did before and would practice self control, pacing myself so I didn't shoot it all in one day. I had a regimen that I stuck with. At least for a little while.

One afternoon, I'd just gotten back from downtown where I scored some powder and black tar. I'd only done the tar once and forgot what it felt like. If there was a chance it was better than the H I'd been getting, then I was all about it. On the way to my room I passed by Dave's old room and caught a glimpse of that military box of his sitting on the floor. I grabbed it and brought it back to my room, then set it on the floor while I pulled out some tin foil I'd gotten from a sub shop dumpster for chasing the tar.

I opened the box and found a ring box inside—the kind you get from a jeweler—and a photograph of a little girl wearing an Easter dress and a wide grin with missing front teeth. She looked about seven or eight years old. I flipped the picture over. On the back, written in pen, it read Ella "Daisy" Bennett with a small flower dotting the "i". I set the picture down and opened the ring box. Inside were four small teeth. They were human teeth but not from an adult. My heart sank and I teared up. I put everything back in the box and slid it across the floor, then reached for my needle. I prepped. I booted. I sank and dreamt, fantasizing of carefree days. Playgrounds and beaches, stardom and wealth.

I gazed at the hallway in front of me. The girl stood beautiful and afraid. Her missing teeth reflecting a profound innocence. I told her I was sorry, that it was never meant to be like this. She shook and cried for hours.

After my nod, I looked out the window next to me. Three kids, not quite in their teens, played with a football in the yard behind the house, the tall grass making small cuts in their legs they wouldn't feel for hours. I broke down and cried. I wanted to jump through the glass and crash below, show them what's waiting for them if they don't keep their shit together. But I didn't. I willed them away and gritted my teeth, then picked up a pencil and started adding flowers to the bare wall.

End

I Believe in Gratitude:

For support and encouragement with this book, thank you: My wife Mary Lutzke, John Boden, Mark Matthews. For beta reading and pointing out ca-ca doo-doo: Matthew Weber, John J. Questore, Robert Pettigrew, Bettina Melher, Derek Bannister, Mark Alan Gunnels, Betty Rocksteady. For my 25+ years of staying clean, thank you: God and His Son, New Day and staff, Aunt Sharon, Sooz, Zombie Aaron and the whole Riverview Mission, my parents, and the Alano Club on Territorial.

Praise for OF FOSTER HOMES AND FLIES

"Original, touching coming of age."
~Jack Ketchum, author of The Girl Next Door

"Disturbing, often gruesome, yet poignant at the same time, Chad Lutzke's OF FOSTER HOMES AND FLIES is one of the best dark coming-of-age tales I've read in years. You'll laugh (sometimes when you know you shouldn't), you'll cry, you'll find yourself

wondering how soon you can read more of this guy's work. Highly recommended!"
~ James Newman, author of MIDNIGHT RAIN, UGLY AS SIN, and ODD MAN OUT

———————

"With OF FOSTER HOMES AND FLIES, Lutzke is firing on all cylinders. It's a lean mean emotional machine. Coming-of-age presented in a fresh direction. Bearing tremendous emotional weight and heart. It made me cry. "
~John Boden, author of JEDI SUMMER.

———————

"OF FOSTER HOMES AND FLIES by Chad Lutzke is a lovely addition to the coming of age subgenre. He creates in the character of Denny an authentic young man with passions and foibles, someone easy to relate to and root for. The novella hits all the right notes you expect out of a coming of age tale, while also providing a plot that has originality and surprises."
~Mark Allan Gunnells, author of FLOWERS IN A DUMPSTER and WHERE THE DEAD GO TO DIE

———————

"...one of those real treats that comes down the pipe and manages to get you all excited about reading again...the whole thing is just beautiful."
~ Ginger Nuts of Horror

Chad lives in Michigan with his wife and children. For over two decades, he has been a contributor to several different outlets in the independent music and film scene, offering articles, reviews, and artwork. He has written for *Famous Monsters of Filmland, Rue Morgue, Cemetery Dance*, and *Scream* magazine. He's had a few dozen stories published, and some of his books include: OF FOSTER HOMES & FLIES, WALLFLOWER, STIRRING THE SHEETS, SKULLFACE BOY, and OUT BEHIND THE BARN co-written with John Boden. Lutzke's work has been praised by authors Jack Ketchum, Stephen Graham Jones, James Newman, and his own mother. He can be found lurking the internet at
www.chadlutzke.com

Manufactured by Amazon.ca
Bolton, ON